My Name Isn't OOF!

Warren the Warbler Takes Flight

MICHAEL GALLIGAN

Illustrated by
JEREMIAH TRAMMELL

little bigfoot
an imprint of sasquatch books
seattle, wa

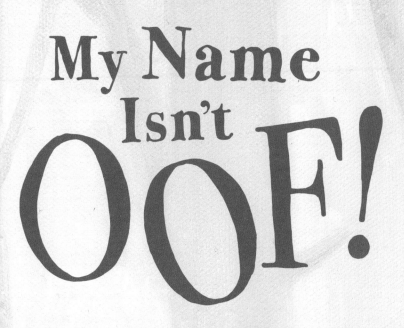

At the edge of a nest, on the brink of a branch,
wobbled a warbler named Warren.

Warren peered at the forest floor far below. His three siblings had just taken flight, each boasting, "I'm flying!"

Now it was his turn. Warren's striped wings trembled. He didn't know if he could do it. But he was a bird after all, so he took a deep breath, shut his eyes, and stepped into the air.
"I'm—"
And he fell.
"Oof!"

Warren sat in a daze atop pine needles and moss. Even his feathers hurt.

A chipmunk bounced over. "Are you OK, Oof? That was quite a crash landing."

"Yes, I think so," Warren said, blinking.

"You forgot to jump," Chipmunk said.

A mouse skittered up.
"What happened to him?"

"Oof forgot to jump," Chipmunk chirped. "Like this."
Chipmunk took a running leap and knocked Mouse
into a mushroom.

"I thought I did jump!" Warren objected. "And my
name isn't Oof!"

A squirrel skipped in.
"What's going on?"

"Oof forgot to jump and spread his wings,"
Mouse squeaked. "Like this." Mouse jumped,
swung her fuzzy arms, and bonked Squirrel in
the nose.

"I thought I did jump and spread my wings,"
Warren protested. "And my name isn't Oof!"

A rabbit hopped over. "What's so serious?"

"Oof forgot to jump, spread his
wings, and flap," Squirrel chittered.
"Like this." Squirrel lost her balance, tripped on
a twig, and bumped Rabbit into a sword fern.

"But I did jump. I did spread my wings. I did flap. Didn't I?"
Warren insisted. "And my name is *not* Oof!"

A skunk waddled up. "What's all the commotion?"

"Oof forgot to jump, spread his wings, and flap. And he
didn't land on his feet," Rabbit reported. "Like this." Rabbit
hopped up, tried to flap his stubby arms, and landed with a
flop on top of Skunk's head.

"Maybe you're right. Maybe I did forget to jump, spread my wings, and flap," Warren admitted. "But that was my first try at flying!"

"It was?" Skunk sniffed.
"And I was scared," Warren said.
"You were?" Chipmunk asked.

"Yes." Warren stood up tall, brushed himself off, and spoke up.
"But now, thanks to all of you, I know I can do it. Like *this*!"
Warren jumped, spread his wings, and flapped hard.

He was in the air! But then, he wobbled.
"Uh-oh!" Skunk said.

Warren swerved toward the ground.
"Look out!" Rabbit cried.

Warren wavered left, then right.
"Take cover!" Squirrel yelled.

Mouse dove under a mushroom, and
Chipmunk scrambled under Skunk's tail.

But Warren kept flapping, and soon he was flying!

"Zee, zee, zee," he warbled with pride.

"He did it!" Chipmunk sang.

Warren circled the others, brushing over them with the tip of his striped wing.

"Hooray for Oof!" everyone cheered.

Warren zoomed past his nest to the top of his tree and sang down to his new friends on the forest floor far below.

"And my name isn't Oof. It's Warren!"

What kind of
bird is Warren?

Warren is a Townsend's Warbler, a small colorful songbird found in the Pacific Northwest. Some will live year-round in the Pacific Northwest and some will migrate between Alaska and Mexico. Townsend's Warblers nest high in the trees of mostly coniferous forests (think evergreen trees with cones, like pine, cedar, spruce, and hemlock) and eat mainly insects.

What should you do
if you find a baby bird?

Once a bird is hatched it is called a hatchling. Hatchlings cannot open their eyes and will have fuzz, called down. Once the baby bird's eyes open, it's called a nestling. A nestling will have a few feathers but cannot flap its wings, hop, or walk, and will look helpless. After a nestling gets larger, stronger, and grows more feathers, it is called a fledgling. A fledgling can hop, walk, and flap its wings. When we meet Warren he is a fledgling, ready to go out on his own.

There are various reasons a baby bird might end up out of its nest. It may get bumped out of a busy nest full of hungry, wriggling babies. It may also try to fly and not make it on its first attempt, like Warren.

If you find a baby bird on the ground, the first thing to do is to determine if it's a hatchling, nestling, or fledgling. If it's a hatchling or nestling you should try to find the nest, which should be close by. Gently return the baby to the nest if you can get to it safely. If you cannot find the nest, or if the nest is in a place you cannot get to safely, provide a small basket or box lined with tissue and put it close to where you found the nestling. Don't try to feed the bird.

If it's a fledgling, the best thing to do is to leave it alone. But if the bird is in a dangerous area, like on or near a road or near pets or predators, then you can move it carefully to a safer area. Keep pets and other people away! Again, don't try to feed the bird.

If the bird seems injured, ask an adult to help you find your local vet or animal rescue/welfare society and alert them. You may have just saved a baby bird!

To Molly: Because of you, our kids will fly. —M.G.

Wolfgang Benjamin and River Leonidas, this one is for you! —J.T.

Copyright © 2019 by Michael Galligan
Illustrations copyright © 2019 by Jeremiah Trammell
Warbler photo © 2019 Jeff Galligan.

Manufactured in China by C&C Offset Printing Co. Ltd. Shenzhen, Guangdong Province, in January 2019

Published by Little Bigfoot, an imprint of Sasquatch Books

LITTLE BIGFOOT with colophon is a registered trademark of Penguin Random House LLC

23 22 21 20 19   9 8 7 6 5 4 3 2 1

Editor: Christy Cox
Design: Tony Ong

Library of Congress Cataloging-in-Publication Data

Names: Galligan, Michael, 1968- author. | Trammell, Jeremiah, illustrator.
Title: My name isn't Oof! : Warren the warbler takes flight / Michael Galligan ; illustrated by Jeremiah Trammell.
Other titles: My name is not Oof!
Description: Seattle, WA : Little Bigfoot, an imprint of Sasquatch Books, [2019] | Summary: The first time Warren, a fledgling bird, leaves the nest he falls straight to the ground, but his fellow forest-dwellers all have advice to share. Includes facts about Townsend Warblers and about baby birds.
Identifiers: LCCN 2018028585 | ISBN 9781632171931 (hardcover)
Subjects: | CYAC: Birds--Fiction. | Flight--Fiction. | Animals--Infancy--Fiction. | Forest animals--Fiction.
Classification: LCC PZ7.1.G34785 My 2019 | DDC [E]--dc23
LC record available at https://lccn.loc.gov/2018028585

ISBN: 978-1-63217-193-1

Sasquatch Books
1904 Third Avenue, Suite 710
Seattle, WA 98101
(206) 467-4300
SasquatchBooks.com

When someone once asked what animal **MICHAEL GALLIGAN** would want to be, he said bird because he thought flying would be the most fantastic ability. Since he still can't fly, he'll settle for watching and listening to the birds on Washington State's Olympic Peninsula, where he lives with his family. *My Name Isn't Oof!* is his authorial debut.

JEREMIAH TRAMMELL is an illustrator whose work has appeared in numerous children's books, including *Little Red Riding Hood of the Pacific Northwest*, *Three Bears of the Pacific Northwest*, and *The Giant Cabbage*. He lives in Seattle.